Food and Garden Waste

Kate Walker

Marshall Cavendish
Benchmark
New York

This edition first published in 2011 in the United States of America by
Marshall Cavendish Benchmark
An imprint of Marshall Cavendish Corporation

Library of Congress Cataloging-in-Publication Data

Walker, Kate.
    Food and garden waste / Kate Walker.
      p. cm. — (Recycling)
    Includes index.
    Summary: "Discusses how food and garden waste is made and the variety of
    ways to recycle it"—Provided by publisher.
    ISBN 978-1-60870-129-2
    1. Refuse and refuse disposal—Juvenile literature. 2. Recycling (Waste,
    etc.)—Juvenile literature. I. Title.
    TD792.W35 2010
    631.8'7—dc22

                                    2009042155

First published in 2009 by
MACMILLAN EDUCATION AUSTRALIAN PTY LTD
15–19 Claremont Street, South Yarra 3141

Visit our website at www.macmillan.com.au or go directly to www.macmillanlibrary.com.au

Associated companies and representatives throughout the world.

Copyright © Kate Walker 2009

Edited by Julia Carlomagno
Text and cover design by Christine Deering
Page layout by Christine Deering
Photo research by Legend Images
Illustrations by Gaston Vanzet

Printed in the United States

Acknowledgments
The author and the publisher are grateful to the following for permission to reproduce copyright material:

Front cover photograph: Two girls recycling waste food courtesy of Coo-ee Picture Library

Photos courtesy of: Coo-ee Picture Library, 1, 12 right, 16, 20, 22, 30; Martin Poole/Getty Images, 12 center; Robert Houser Photography, 28, 29; © Micha Adamczyk/iStockphoto, 7 top right; © Ian Francis/iStockphoto, 13 right; © Peter Garbet/iStockphoto, 21; © gremlin/iStockphoto, 18; © Ralph125/ iStockphoto, 5; © Vasiliy Yakobchuk/iStockphoto, 7 top center; © CIN, Geoff Bryant, Natural Sciences Image Library, 8; Photographer G. R. "Dick" Roberts © Natural Sciences Image Library, 13 left; © Peter E. Smith, Natural Sciences Image Library, 12 left, 15, 23, 30; © Newspix / News Ltd /Guy Thayer, 14; Photolibrary © Don Smith/Alamy, 4; Photolibrary/Big Cheese, 9; © Victoria Alexandrova/Shutterstock, 7 bottom left; © Donald Barger/ Shutterstock, 3, 17; © Sascha Burkard/Shutterstock, 7 bottom right; © clearviewstock/Shutterstock, 30; © Gertjan Hooijer/Shutterstock, 7 bottom center; © Oneuser/Shutterstock, 7 top left; © Kiselev Andrey Valerevich/Shutterstock, 6; West Leeming Primary School, 26, 27.

While every care has been taken to trace and acknowledge copyright, the publisher tenders their apologies for any accidental infringement where copyright has proved untraceable. Where the attempt has been unsuccessful, the publisher welcomes information that would redress the situation.

1 3 5 6 4 2

Contents

What Is Recycling?	4
Food Products and Food Waste	6
Garden Plants and Garden Waste	8
Throwing Away or Recycling Food and Garden Waste?	10
How Food and Garden Waste Is Recycled	12
Recycling Food Waste in a Worm Farm	14
Recycling Garden Waste in a Compost Heap	16
Can All Food Waste Be Recycled?	18
Is Recycling Food and Garden Waste the Best Option?	20
Reducing Food Waste	22
Make a Worm-Watch Jar	24
School Recycling Projects	26
How Recycling Food Helps Animals	30
Glossary	31
Index	32

Glossary Words
When a word is printed in **bold**, you can look up its meaning in the Glossary on page 31.

What Is Recycling?

Recycling is collecting used products and making them into new products. Recycling is easy and keeps the environment clean.

Recycling food scraps helps the environment.

Why Recycle Food and Garden Waste?

Recycling food and garden waste helps:

- save **natural resources** for future use
- reduce **pollution** in the environment
- keep waste material out of **landfills**

If more food and garden waste was recycled, landfills such as this one could be closed.

Food Products and Food Waste

All the food products we eat come from plants and animals. Food products we get from plants include:

- fruit and vegetables
- grains, nuts, and seeds

Food products we get from animals include:

- meat and fish
- eggs, milk, and cheese

All of the fresh food products we eat come from animals or plants.

Food Waste

Food waste comes from those parts of plants and animals that we cannot eat. Food is also wasted when it gets too old to eat.

banana skins

eggshells

meat and fish bones

stale bread

moldy cheese

old fruit and vegetables

Garden Plants and Garden Waste

Gardens can have many different kinds of plants.
Garden plants include:

- trees
- bushes
- grass
- flowers
- vegetables

You can grow lots of different kinds of plants in a garden.

Garden Waste

All garden plants produce garden waste.
Garden waste includes:

- dead leaves from trees
- prunings from bushes
- grass cuttings from lawns
- dead flowers or vegetables
- unwanted plants, such as weeds

Gardens grow best when plants are cut back and garden waste is removed.

Throwing Away or Recycling Food and Garden Waste?

Throwing away food and garden waste uses natural resources, increases pollution, and adds to waste.

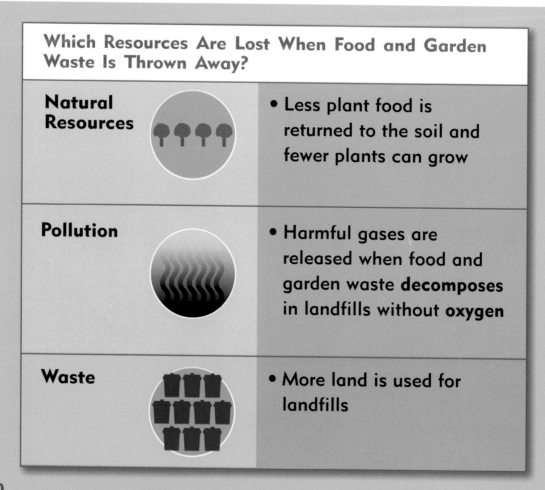

Which Resources Are Lost When Food and Garden Waste Is Thrown Away?

Natural Resources		• Less plant food is returned to the soil and fewer plants can grow
Pollution		• Harmful gases are released when food and garden waste **decomposes** in landfills without **oxygen**
Waste		• More land is used for landfills

Recycling food and garden waste saves natural resources, cuts down pollution, and reduces waste. Which do you think is better, throwing away or recycling food and garden waste?

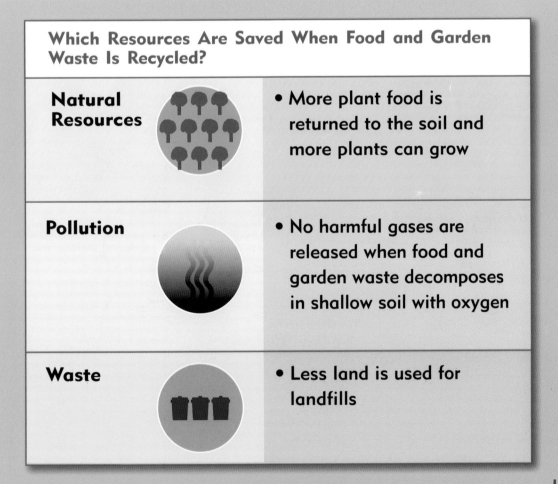

Which Resources Are Saved When Food and Garden Waste Is Recycled?

Natural Resources		• More plant food is returned to the soil and more plants can grow
Pollution		• No harmful gases are released when food and garden waste decomposes in shallow soil with oxygen
Waste		• Less land is used for landfills

How Food and Garden Waste Is Recycled

Food and garden waste is recycled through a five-stage **process**. This process begins when we recycle used food and garden waste. It ends with plant food.

  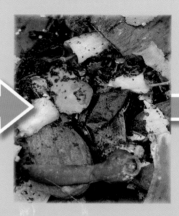

Stage 1
Food waste is collected from kitchens. Garden waste is gathered from gardens.

Stage 2
Food and garden waste is put into **worm farms** or **compost heaps**.

Stage 3
Inside worm farms and compost heaps, the waste decomposes. **Micro-organisms** break down the waste material into tiny particles and eat it.

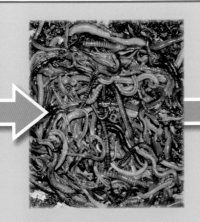

Stage 4

Micro-organisms and worms leave droppings in the soil. These droppings are decomposed waste.

Stage 5

Decomposed waste is added to garden soil to feed growing plants. Plants absorb it through their roots.

Recycling Food Waste in a Worm Farm

Food waste can be recycled at home and at school in a worm farm. A worm farm is a closed box containing moist soil, **organic material**, and worms.

Large worm farms at schools may contain hundreds of worms.

Food waste decomposes quickly in a worm farm. Worms have plenty to eat so they grow fast and breed more worms. More worms eat more waste.

Liquid worm droppings, or worm castings, collect in a tray and make great plant food.

Recycling Garden Waste in a Compost Heap

Garden waste can be recycled at home or at school in a compost heap. A compost heap is a mix of soil and garden waste piled together on the ground or in a compost bin.

Garden waste can be recycled in a compost bin.

Garden waste decomposes slowly in a compost heap. Garden waste includes a lot of weeds and leaves. Micro-organisms and worms take longer to break down tough plants and leaves.

A compost heap produces a dark, crumbly material called compost, or humus.

Can All Food Waste Be Recycled?

All food waste can be recycled. However, some food waste causes problems in worm farms and compost heaps. Worms cannot eat oil or **citrus fruit**. Meat and dairy products attract pests such as cockroaches.

Meat scraps should go in the trash can.

Many types of food waste can be recycled in worm farms or compost heaps. It is good to recycle these types of food waste.

Which Types of Food Waste Can Be Recycled in Worm Farms and Compost Heaps?	
Materials recycled in worm farms	**Materials recycled in compost heaps**
✓ fruit and vegetable scraps	✓ fruit and vegetable scraps
✓ bread and grains	✓ bread and grains
✓ tea bags	✓ tea bags
✓ eggshells	✓ eggshells

Is Recycling Food and Garden Waste the Best Option?

Food and garden waste should always be recycled. When the waste is buried in landfills it gives off methane gas. Methane gas adds to **global warming**.

Global warming is making some parts of the planet too dry to grow food.

Food and garden waste can also be recycled as mulch. Mulch is a layer of plant waste laid on top of soil to keep moisture in. Mulch helps plants to grow.

Grass cuttings and shredded leaves make good mulch.

Reducing Food Waste

There are many ways to reduce food waste. One way is to buy only as much fresh food as is needed for the next few days.

Some shoppers figure out how many fresh fruits and vegetables they need to buy.

Some simple ways to reduce food waste are:

- check use-by date labels on food products at home, to make sure food is eaten before it **expires**
- buy small amounts of food you haven't tried before in case you do not like them
- store leftover food in airtight containers for later use

Store leftover salad in an airtight container to eat at a later time.

Make a Worm-Watch Jar

Worms help food and garden waste decompose.
Make a worm-watch jar to watch worms at work.

What You Will Need:

- a large, clear glass jar
- a plastic lid for the jar with ten holes punched into it
- moist soil
- moist sand washed to remove salt
- uncooked rolled oats
- about ten earthworms

What to Do:

1. Put 1 inch (2 cm) of moist soil in the jar, followed by a teaspoon of rolled oats. Add 1 inch (2 cm) of moist sand, then a teaspoon of rolled oats.

2. Repeat this process until the jar is filled. End with soil on top.

3. Place earthworms in the jar and screw on the lid. Cover the jar with a cloth and move it away from direct sunlight. Make sure the soil stays moist.

4. After a week see how the worms have moved the soil and sand around while searching for food. Then carefully return the worms to a worm farm or garden bed.

School Recycling Projects

West Leeming Primary School in Western Australia recycles all fruit and vegetable scraps. The teachers' lounge, school cafeterias, and classrooms all have buckets for collecting food waste.

Fruit and vegetable scraps are added to the school's worm farms and compost bins every day.

Students use worm castings and compost as **fertilizer** in school gardens. Unused fertilizer and compost are sold to parents.

Students grow vegetables using liquid worm fertilizer, made from lunch leftovers.

School Recycling Projects

In 2009 students at Beach School in California watched food waste turn into compost. They put food scraps, paper plates, compost, and five live worms into a clear plastic box.

Students put food scraps, compost, and worms into the box.

The students watched the level of stuff inside the box drop lower each week. By the end of semester the food scraps and paper plates had turned into compost. There were more than twenty worms.

All food scraps and paper waste inside the box turned into compost.

How Recycling Food and Garden Waste Helps Animals

When food and garden waste is returned to the soil it feeds many animals living there. When you recycle food and garden waste you help many animals, including:

- earthworms

- ground beetles

- centipedes

Glossary

citrus fruit   Juicy fruit that you must peel to eat, such as lemons and oranges.

compost heaps   Piles of moist soil and decomposing waste.

decomposes   Breaks down into tiny particles.

expires   Becomes too old to eat safely.

fertilizer   Food for plants.

global warming   Heating up of Earth's atmosphere.

landfills   Large holes in the ground where garbage is buried.

micro-organisms   Tiny living creatures.

natural resources   Materials found in nature that people use and value.

organic material   Matter that was part of a living thing.

oxygen   A gas needed by many living things.

pollution   Waste that damages the air, water, or land.

process   A series of actions that brings about a change.

worm farms   Boxes in which earthworms live and feed, producing worm castings and compost.

Index

A

animals, 6, 7, 30
apple cores, 29

C

compost, 12, 16, 17, 26, 27,
    28
compost bins, 16
compost heaps, 12, 16–17,
    18, 19

D

dairy products, 18
decompose, 10, 11, 12, 13,
    15, 17, 24

E

expire, 23

F

fertilizer, 27
food waste, 5, 6–7, 10, 11,
    12–15, 18–23, 24, 26, 30
fruit, 6, 7, 18, 22, 28
fruit scraps, 19, 26, 28

G

garden waste, 5, 8–13, 16–17,
    20–21, 24, 28–29, 30

H

humus, 17

L

landfills, 5, 10, 11, 20

M

meat, 6, 7, 18
methane gas, 20
micro-organisms, 12, 13, 17
mulch 21

N

natural resources, 5, 10, 11

O

organic material, 14
oxygen, 10, 11

P

plant food, 10, 11, 12, 13, 15
plants, 6, 7, 8, 9, 10, 11, 13,
    17, 21, 28
pollution, 5, 10, 11

V

vegetables, 6, 7, 8, 9, 19, 22,
    27

W

worm castings, 15, 27
worm farms, 12, 13, 14–15,
    18, 19, 25, 26
worm-watch jar, 24–25